A catalogue record for this book is available from the British Library

Published by Ladybird Books Ltd
80 Strand London WC2R 0RL
A Penguin Company

4 6 8 10 9 7 5 3

© Ladybird Books Ltd MMVI

ISBN-13: 978-1-84422-951-2
ISBN-10: 1-84422-951-3

Printed in Italy

Clever Car

written by Jillian Harker
illustrated by Ruth Galloway

It's early in the morning and the curtains are still closed in most of the houses on Cranbrook Road. But not at number forty-six. Someone has already opened the garage doors there. A bright blue car waits inside, with a shiny bonnet and gleaming hub caps. Clever Car is ready to start the day.

Suddenly, the front door opens. Joe and his mum and dad rush into the garage. *Clunk!* go three of Clever Car's doors as they jump in. *Vrooom!* roars the lively engine. Dad mustn't miss his train, Clever Car!

Of course, Clever Car gets him to the station just in time.

Clever Car revs up again. It's time to take Joe to school. *Left!* flick the indicators. *Right!* they flash. *Left!* they signal again, as Clever Car twists and turns.

Joe gets to school right on time.
Make sure the hand brake is on,
Clever Car!

As usual, it's one job after another for Clever Car. Now, it's time to get Mum to work.

Oh dear, it looks as if there are no parking spaces! But Clever Car doesn't give up easily.

Look, there's one space left.
Into reverse gear! Hard left with
the steering wheel, hard right
with the steering wheel!

Clever Car just manages to fit in.

Soon after lunch, Clever Car is on the move again. Mum has finished work and needs to do the family shopping. Clever Car gets her to the supermarket in no time at all.

And after the game, there's a full load for Clever Car to bring home. It's Joe's friends, who are coming back for tea. They mustn't forget to put their seat belts on!

Clever Car still has one trip to make today, to the petrol station.

Off with the petrol cap. *Glug! Glug!* Fill up the thirsty tank. It's the weekend tomorrow and Clever Car is going to need plenty of fuel.

It's back home next to unload the shopping but Clever Car can't stay still for long. Here comes Joe with his football kit. He's trusting Clever Car to get him to his practice.

It's Saturday at last! Clever Car and the family are off to the seaside. It feels good to have the windows wide open and to let the warm air rush in.

Clever Car purrs through the countryside towards the sea.

There's not much traffic on the country roads. Now Clever Car can cruise along. But there is one very steep hill. Hard work here for the gear stick!

At last, Clever Car drives over the top of the hill. The open road reaches ahead. The sea stretches out in the distance. This is the way to travel!

So does Clever Car get a well-earned rest by the sea? The engine is quiet. The hand brake is on. The gears are in neutral. But now Clever Car has other jobs to do...

as a changing room, a picnic
table and a treasure chest!

And when darkness falls, Clever Car will still be ready.

Headlights on? Clever Car zooms off home.